The Zoo in Willy's Bed

Written and Illustrated by
Kate Sturman Gorman

My little brother Willy has a zoo in his bed.

He has a lion.

He has a frog.

He has three bears.

And he has a monkey.

Willy is the zookeeper.

At night Willy tucks the animals in bed.

He pats lion.

He hugs frog.

He sings to the bears and hugs them too.

He kisses monkey.

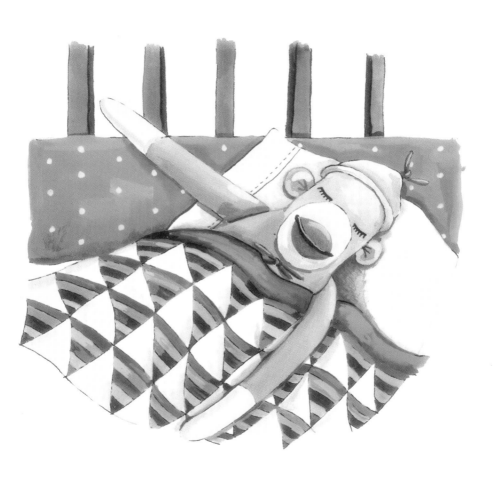

But monkey is asleep.

Then Willy gets his hug and kiss.

And I do too.

Goodnight zoo.
Goodnight zookeeper.
Time to go to sleep.